Snow White

STERLING CHILDREN'S BOOKS
New York

FROM A FAIRY TALE BY THE
Brothers Grimm

TEXT ADAPTATION GIADA FRANCIA • GRAPHIC DESIGN MARINELLA DEBERNARDI

ILLUSTRATIONS BY
Francesca Rossi

It was a frosty winter's morning and the snowflakes were falling gently. The queen was sitting alone by the window, embroidering. But she was not thinking about her work. Her mind was wandering. For some time the king and queen had wanted to have a child, but no baby had arrived. That morning the queen daydreamed about how her life might be if one day her desire were fulfilled.

Lost in thought, she accidentally pricked her finger, and a drop of blood fell onto the cloth. As she watched the red drop soak into the white fabric, a thought came to her: *I would like a child with lips as red as this drop of blood, hair as black as coal, and skin as white as snow.*

Perhaps some good fairy heard the queen's wish, because it was not long before it came true. A child was born, and the queen called her Snow White. Unfortunately, the queen was stricken with an unknown illness soon after. No one could help her: neither the doctors summoned from all over the kingdom, nor the wise men who came from faraway lands. Soon, they lost all hope of saving her.

For months, the king grieved with his baby daughter. But he had many duties to perform, and very soon the kingdom could do without him no longer. He realized that he would have to leave Snow White alone at the palace for months at a time, and so he made a decision. He would marry again, so that the girl would have a mother, even though he knew that no one could ever take the place of his beloved queen.

He wed his new bride on a cold autumn morning. When their carriage returned to the palace, a crowd awaited, eager to glimpse their new queen. A tall and elegant woman stepped out of the carriage, pushing back the hood of her cloak to reveal shining hair and a beautiful face. An awed hush fell over the crowd. Grimhilde—for that was her name—smiled to see everyone's reaction to her incredible beauty. She curtsied to the crowd and went into the castle, followed by two footmen carefully carrying a large and heavy crate.

Many hours later, when she was finally alone in her room, Grimhilde went across to the mysterious crate. With a single grand gesture, she threw aside the material it was wrapped in. She opened the crate to reveal a mirror. As she gazed at her reflection, an incredible thing happened. Little by little, her face changed. Her hair transformed into long feathers, and a beak stuck out in place of her delicate profile. The queen had changed into a crow! Grimhilde was really a powerful witch, but no one knew of her powers, among which was the magic mirror that accompanied her wherever she went. She turned to the mirror and spoke.

"*Mirror, mirror on the wall, who's the fairest of them all?*"

At this, the mirror came alive. The reflection in the glass began to swirl around until it took the form of a face. The face replied: "My queen, in all the kingdom there is none more beautiful than you."

Every evening, Grimhilde consulted the mirror, and every time she heard the same reply. Reassured, she would turn back into the splendid queen, whom everyone admired for her beauty. No one suspected that she could possess such evil powers.

The years passed, and Snow White's eighteenth birthday arrived. As she grew, the young woman had become more like her mother. She had inherited her kindness, gaiety, and real beauty.

On the morning of her birthday, Snow White ran into the garden. She had spent hours with her maids and her dressmaker, getting ready for her birthday party, and she needed a breath of fresh air.

Hearing laughter, the stepmother went out onto the terrace, and what she saw took her breath away.

Snow White looked enchanting. She was wearing the dress chosen for her party. It sparkled with sequins that lit up her eyes. With her hair arranged elegantly and her cheeks shining in the fresh air, she no longer seemed like the child who played in the woods with a mud-spattered skirt. For the first time, the queen realized that the little girl had become a very beautiful young woman.

"She's graceful, but she is certainly not more beautiful than I!" she exclaimed. "There is no woman in the world more beautiful than I!"

The queen hurried back to her room. There was only one way to know the truth.

"Mirror, mirror on the wall, who's the fairest of them all? Mirror, I order you to tell me the truth, or I will smash you to smithereens!"

"Your Majesty, I cannot lie, and I'm afraid that for this you will smash me to smithereens," replied the mirror.

"What do you mean?" demanded the stepmother.

"You will not be happy with what I am going to say. Your Majesty, you are beautiful, but there is Snow White, and she is more beautiful than you," whispered the mirror.

At these words, the queen shrieked. Just as Grimhilde was about to smash the mirror, she came up with an idea.

"I still need you," she said. "You will once again tell me that I am the most beautiful."

"I cannot lie. While Snow White still lives, you will never be the most beautiful in the kingdom."

"As you said yourself, while Snow White still *lives*. I have no intention of allowing a mere girl to take my place! I will stop at nothing!" declared the stepmother.

When the castle awoke after the princess's party, the queen summoned the royal huntsman. "Huntsman, come near," she said as he entered her chambers. "I have a special task. A task that only a very brave man can do, and they tell me that you are he."

"Surely, I—"

"I hope that you are also discreet. What I am about to tell you must remain between us. Do I have your word that you will speak of this to no one?"

"My queen. Give me the word and I will do anything you ask!"

"I will give you three words," whispered Grimhilde. "Kill Snow White!"

"What!"

"Take her into the woods today, and make it look like there was an accident during one of your usual walks. Then bring me her heart in this casket!" added the stepmother, putting a jewel box into the huntsman's hands. "Will you do as I ask?"

The huntsman was speechless. He was silent for a long time, and then whispered, "I will obey, my queen."

Snow White liked the idea of going into the woods. The girl chattered about the party the night before, and couldn't stop talking about the charming prince she had met.

The huntsman, however, walked with his head down, with only one thought: he must kill Snow White. But how could he ever do so? He knew that the queen would not spare his life if he failed, and so . . .

He gripped the handle of his hunting knife so hard it hurt his fingers. Slowly, he pulled the knife out. Snow White turned and saw the knife in the huntsman's hand and the tears that streamed down his cheeks.

"I can't! My child, I can't harm you!"

"What are you saying? What's happening?"

The man fell to his knees and confessed everything.

"My stepmother? I . . . I don't believe it!" exclaimed Snow White.

"You must, my child! This woman is evil and will stop at nothing to destroy you!" said the huntsman.

"But where shall I go?" asked Snow White, weeping.

"Where doesn't matter, child! But go now! Run!" cried the huntsman.

Snow White embraced him, wiped away her tears, and whispered, "Farewell." Then she turned and fled.

The huntsman watched her go, then went further into the woods. When he saw a wild boar, he took out his bow and killed it. He put the animal's heart into the jewel box, then turned and made for the palace. The queen was waiting impatiently.

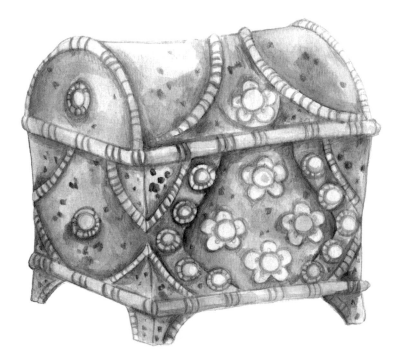

"Well?" she asked, when he arrived in her chambers. "Have you done what I ordered?"

"Yes, Your Majesty. You no longer need to worry about Snow White." He put the box into Grimhilde's hands. When she opened it, she began to laugh uncontrollably.

"It's done! Congratulations, my faithful huntsman. I wish to reward you! What would you like? Money?"

"I would like to go hunting beyond the mountains."

"Granted, you may go."

While the huntsman was leaving the palace never to return, Snow White was about to face the most frightening night of her life. The princess had never seen the woods by night, and she would never have believed that the same trees she climbed by day could become so scary when darkness fell. The branches seemed like monstrous arms ready to grab at her, and the noises of the night creatures sounded like muffled laughter.

The next morning, after hours of running without knowing where she was going, Snow White finally stumbled upon a cottage. It was in the middle of a clearing in the depths of the woods.

"I will ask the people inside for shelter," said Snow White. She went up to the door and knocked timidly. "Is there anybody there? May I come in?"

There was no reply, so she tried knocking harder. The door, which was not locked, opened slightly. Snow White bent down to go through the low entrance and went into the cottage. A fireplace was gently crackling with flames, but the room was empty.

"Perhaps I could just wait by the fire until the owner comes back. It would be far better than going back into woods!" she said to herself with a shiver. She plucked up her courage and closed the little door behind her. As Snow White looked around the room, she stared open-mouthed at what she saw.

Everything in the room seemed to have been magically miniaturized. There was a table set with seven little plates. The cutlery was tiny, and so were the bread rolls. Passing

through the room, she saw tiny cups on the dresser that reminded her of her dolls' tea set. She noticed a stack of small books that seemed to be well thumbed.

"Whoever lives in this house is a lover of literature," she said to herself. Then she saw a little flute and a chisel on a seat. "There must also be a musician and a sculptor. How strange," murmured the girl, yawning. Then she saw a staircase leading to the floor above. "I wonder if there is anyone up there?"

But when she went up, she found only seven small beds. She squeezed into one of them and dozed off. Snow White slept the entire day, and was still in bed when the inhabitants of the cottage returned.

It was seven dwarfs. They were returning from the mine where they went every day to dig for precious gems.

The seven dwarfs had come home looking forward to a good long sleep. They certainly did not expect to find a beautiful girl in one of their beds.

"She's as beautiful as a fairy!" whispered one of the dwarfs. "Do you think she is one?"

"I think she's a stranger who's trespassing in my bed!" replied another, annoyed.

"Shh! Don't shout! You'll wake her up."

"To tell you the truth, I'm already awake," said Snow White, opening her eyes.

"Oh! Hello! Come. Here, have a seat," the eldest dwarf offered. "You mustn't be frightened. We won't hurt you. What's your name?"

"Snow White. I'm sorry to have come into your house without asking, but I didn't know where else to go. I . . . I no longer have a home," she concluded, her eyes bright with tears.

"So stay here!" proposed a smiling dwarf.

Snow White felt safe for the first time in many hours. She could not have imagined that the queen had discovered the truth . . .

Back at the palace, Grimhilde asked her magic mirror if she was now the fairest one of all. The mirror replied:

"You are the most beautiful within the palace walls. But Snow White is still alive, and she is more beautiful than you."

"But that's impossible!" cried the stepmother. "The huntsman killed Snow White! Show her to me!"

In the mirror appeared a laughing Snow White, surrounded by seven woodland dwarfs. Grimhilde went pale and did not know what to say.

"The huntsman lied to me!" she cried. "There is nothing for it. I will see to Snow White myself."

Grimhilde darted from the room and ran down to the palace cellars, where she had hidden her books of black magic. She worked for the rest of the night, looking for a spell that would rid her of the princess once and for all. Then she prepared a magic potion and drank it. As she started transforming, she dropped the flask of potion and hissed:

*"This time,
Snow White
will not escape!"*

The next morning the dwarfs left to work in the mine. Snow White was all alone in the cottage when she heard a voice outside. She went to the window and saw an old dressmaker approaching. The woman had a basket that overflowed with splendid fabrics.

"Good day, my pretty. I'm selling rich cloth from faraway lands. May I come in?" she said with a smile.

Snow White looked at the old dressmaker. There was something familiar about her. But she seemed harmless, so Snow White let her in. The old woman pulled a long satin ribbon from her basket.

"Let's tie this around your waist. You'll see how much better you look!"

Snow White went to her and the old woman knotted the ribbon, then started to pull it tight.

"Wait, I can't breathe!" gasped Snow White before falling to the floor.

The stepmother, disguised as an old dressmaker, tried to hide her wicked grin. She did not see that the woodland creatures ran to the dwarfs' mine to alert them.

"Oh dear! Let me help you up," Grimhilde offered. As she talked, she took a comb out of her pocket. It was a magic comb that poisoned whomever it touched.

What a marvelous comb! thought Snow White, enchanted.

"It will make your hair shiny and soft. Let me show you."

Grimhilde went up to Snow White and started to comb her long black hair. A single touch of the comb was enough. Snow White fell to the ground unconscious. Grimhilde's dress changed color and her hair stood on end as she cackled with delight.

Before Grimhilde could do anything further, she heard noises outside. It was the seven dwarfs racing to the cottage. The woodland creatures had alerted them of danger, and they were returning hastily. Grimhilde quickly transformed herself into a crow and flew back to the palace.

The eldest dwarf was the first to reach the cottage. He pulled the poisoned comb out of the princess's hair, saving her life. Slowly, she began to stir. The dwarfs surrounded Snow White and helped her up. She explained to them what had happened.

"Snow White, you took a great risk!" said one of the dwarfs.

"We will stay with you today," said another.

"I'm fine!" reassured Snow White. "It's nothing, really. Let's not talk about this mysterious lady anymore. Please don't let me interfere with your work. You must return to the mine."

"Very well, but don't trust anyone," warned the eldest dwarf.

The dwarfs left the cottage, leaving Snow White by herself.

Meanwhile, back in her chambers, Grimhilde consulted her mirror.

"Mirror, mirror on the wall, who's the fairest of them all?"

The mirror replied, "You are fair, my queen. But Snow White remains with the seven dwarfs, and she is still the fairest in all the lands."

Grimhilde clenched her fists in rage. She was determined this time to use her darkest arts, creating a terrible spell from which Snow White would not escape. She spent all night in the palace cellars working on a dark concoction.

When the potion was ready, the witch took an apple and dipped it into the smoking liquid. Then she transformed herself into an old fruit seller and set out for the cottage.

At the cottage, Snow White decided to do something to repay her new friends' kindness and hospitality. She spent the afternoon sweeping and cleaning the cottage. Once the place was spotless, she decided to bake a pie for the dwarfs. Snow White was certain they would enjoy such a treat after a long day at the mine. She gathered ingredients from the small kitchen, and soon realized there was little for the filling.

"How can you make a pie without any fruit?" she wondered aloud. As soon as she spoke, she heard a voice calling outside.

"Apples! Red, juicy apples!"

An old woman was coming along carrying a basket full of the most beautiful apples Snow White had ever seen. They would be perfect for her pie. She called the old fruit seller to her.

"It's your lucky day, my dear. These apples are delicious. Here, try one. See how you like it!"

She offered Snow White the reddest and shiniest apple in the basket. The girl bit into it and her head immediately started swimming.

Snow White fell to the floor and everything went dark.

"This time, no one can save you!" Grimhilde cackled.

The dwarfs were returning from the mine just as the old fruit seller came out of the cottage. Before they could say anything, she took a great leap and turned into a crow. The shiny black bird let out a haunting caw as it flew into the distance.

The dwarfs hurried in through the open door and saw Snow White on the ground, the apple sitting next to her body. They gently shook her and splashed cold water on

her face. They tried everything to wake the girl, but eventually they realized there was no cure. Snow White was lifeless.

"My friends, the princess will sleep forever. There's nothing we can do," sobbed the eldest dwarf.

The seven dwarfs grieved for a long time. Then they made a decision. They would lay their friend on a crystal bed in the middle of the clearing. For days they carved the rock without resting. When the shrine was ready, they placed the young sleeping girl in it and surrounded her with woodland flowers.

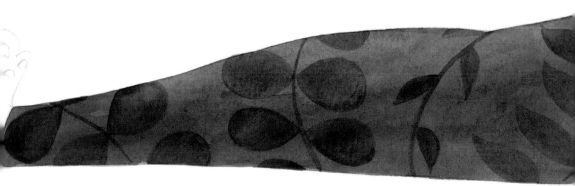

The summer passed and autumn arrived, but Snow White did not wake up. Then one day, when the dwarfs came home from work, they saw something unexpected. Next to the crystal bed stood a young prince. He had been out riding when he came upon the clearing.

"Stop there! Don't you dare touch her!" shouted a dwarf.

"I mean her no harm, I assure you," said the young man, without raising his eyes from the enigmatic beauty that had enchanted him.

"I . . . I know this young woman," he added. "She's a princess. I met her at her birthday party. It seems so long ago. Since then I haven't been able to get her out of my mind! Is she asleep?"

"She has fallen under an evil spell," explained the eldest dwarf. "She's been asleep for months, and there's no way of waking her. But why are you smiling?"

"I recall a fairy tale that I was often told when I was a child. A king is woken from a witch's spell by the kiss of a woodland fairy. Perhaps it's worth trying."

The prince went up to Snow White and placed a kiss delicately onto her red lips. The dwarfs were astonished to see Snow White move slightly. First, she smiled. Then her eyelids fluttered open, and at last she turned to look at the prince.

"I know you," she whispered.

The dwarfs jumped for joy. Snow White was awake! The prince, smiling, took her hand and asked her to come back to his castle as his bride.

"I will go with you," said Snow White, "because I love you more than any other, and because I will never be safe in my kingdom. The fruit seller was my stepmother! I recognized her laugh before I fainted."

"We saw her come out of the house and change herself into a crow," exclaimed one of the dwarfs. "I think it's time to put that evil bird in a cage!"

"Yes!" the other dwarfs cried in unison. They hurried to the castle, where they found the king. He had returned from the farthest reaches of his kingdom. The huntsman had warned him of the stepmother's evil intentions and the danger in which his daughter found herself. Enraged, the king had returned to the castle as quickly as possible and had sought out the queen. She had tried to flee by turning herself into a crow, but the huntsman had caught the bird. They locked Grimhilde in a gilded cage, from which she would never be able to escape.

"She will never again harm my daughter!" said the king. "But now take me to Snow White, I beg you!"

When Snow White saw her father in the clearing, she ran to him and embraced him, crying. "Today is the best day of my life. At last, I can embrace you again! And may I introduce you to someone?"

The prince bowed to the king and explained that he intended to wed Snow White.

"This is a splendid day. Not only have I found my daughter, but I have also met her future husband! When shall we have the wedding?" asked the king.

"As soon as we get back to the palace," said Snow White, with a smile.

STERLING CHILDREN'S BOOKS
New York

An Imprint of Sterling Publishing
387 Park Avenue South
New York, NY 10016

STERLING CHILDREN'S BOOKS and the distinctive Sterling
Children's Books logo are registered trademarks of Sterling
Publishing Co., Inc.

First Sterling edition 2015
First published in Italy in 2014 by De Agostini Libri S.p.A.

© 2014 De Agostini Libri S.p.A.

ISBN 978-1-4549-1513-3

Distributed in Canada by Sterling Publishing
c/o Canadian Manda Group, 165 Dufferin Street
Toronto, Ontario, Canada M6K 3H6
For information about custom editions, special sales,
and premium and corporate purchases,
please contact Sterling Special Sales at 800-805-5489
or specialsales@sterlingpublishing.com.

Translation: Contextus s.r.l., Pavia, Italy (Louise Bostock)
Editor: Contextus s.r.l., Pavia, Italy (Martin Maguire)

Manufactured in China
Lot #:
2 4 6 8 10 9 7 5 3 1
11/14
www.sterlingpublishing.com/kids